THUNDER TRUCK!

MONSTER TRUCK MYTHS

BY BLAKE HOENA

ILLUSTRATED BY FERN CANO

D0972989

Capstone Young Readers
a capstone imprint

ThunderTrucks! is published by
Stone Arch Books
a Capstone imprint
1710 Roe Crest Drive
North Mankato, Minnesota 56003
www.mycapstone.com

Cataloging-in-Publication Data is available on the
Library of Congress website.

ISBN: 978-1-68436-000-0 (paperback)
ISBN: 978-1-68436-001-7 (eBook)

Designed by Brann Garvey

Printed and bound in China.
010736S18

CONTENTS

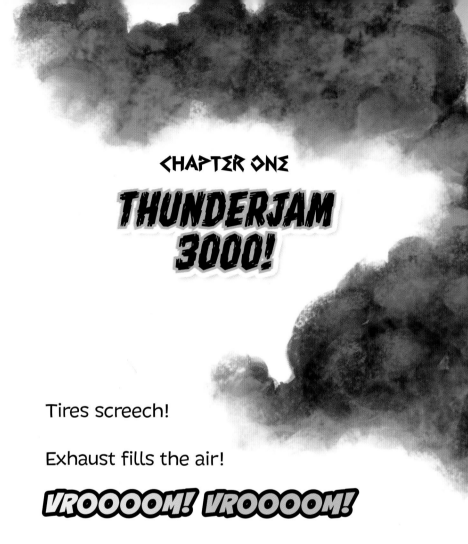

CHAPTER ONE

THUNDERJAM 3000!

Tires screech!

Exhaust fills the air!

VROOOOM! VROOOOM!

Inside a giant arena, a sellout crowd

of monster trucks revs their engines

with excitement.

A new truck named Theseus parks among the fully fueled fans. He's there to watch the annual **ThunderJam 3000!**

Every year, the biggest, loudest ThunderTrucks on Earth compete in three death-defying events.

"Next up," an announcer roars, "ten-time tire-jumping champion . . . **PERSEUS!**"

The crowd flashes their high beams with delight. The sky-blue ThunderTruck rolls to the starting line. His custom, winged paint job glitters in their headlights.

Without delay, Perseus puts pedal to metal and speeds toward a ramp.

FWOOOOSH!

The high-flying ThunderTruck soars over a long row of flaming tires. He lands safely on the other side with a massive

THUMP!

"Ninety tires!" the announcer booms.

BEEP! BEEP! BEEP!

The crowd gives three honks for their champion.

Just then, Theseus spots something in his rearview mirror. "Look!" the rookie truck cries out.

A giant, flame-red monster truck rumbles into the arena and revs its engine.

Thick, black smoke spews from two horn-shaped pipes on the vehicle's hood.

"Ladies and gentletrucks, we have one final competitor," the announcer sputters with fear. **"BULLISTIC!"**

The megaton monster truck hits the gas and spins circles at the starting line. A cloud of dust spills onto the crowd. **"COUGH! COUGH!"** Theseus' air filter clogs with grit and grime. His windshield cakes with mud. "I can't see!" he shouts, turning his wipers on high.

When the dust finally clears, Bullistic is parked at the end of an impossibly long row of flaming tires.

"One hundred tires!" the announcer calls out. "That's a new ThunderJam record, folks!"

Happy honks fills the arena.

"Huh?" Theseus exclaims.

Did anytruck actually see Bullistic jump those tires? the rookie truck wonders.

Before Theseus can argue with the results, the next competition begins.

"Prepare yourselves," the announcer booms, "for the . . .

RUMMMMBBBLE!

A deep rumbling fills the arena. The
asphalt beneath the spectators' tires begins
to quake and crack.

A hulking, golden ThunderTruck enters
the arena.

"HERCULES! HERCULES!"

everytruck chants.

VROOM! VROOM! VROOM!

Hercules revs his engine, and his lion-shaped hood roars with maximum horsepower. He lines up on the far side of a bubbling mud pit and awaits a challenger.

The other ThunderTrucks know Hercules can't be beat. One by one, they turn off their engines — except Bullistic.

The evil monster truck parks on the opposite side of the mud pit.

SNORT! SNORT!

Angry flames explode from Bullistic's horn-shaped pipes.

A ThunderJam official hooks a heavy chain to the front bumper of each competitor. On the count of three, the trucks will tug each other toward the pit, and the loser will get a bubbling mud bath.

"One!" shouts the announcer.

Hercules' engine rumbles. A wicked smile appears on Bullistic's front grill.

"Two!" the announcer continues.

Just then, Bullistic lets out a deafening blare from his bullhorn.

SNNOOOORRTT!

No truck, including Hercules, hears the announcer yell, ***"Three!"*** But that doesn't stop Bullistic. The evil monster truck shifts into reverse, spins his tires, and pulls Hercules into the pit of mud.

SHLOOOP!!

"And the winner is . . . **BULLISTIC!**" the announcer proclaims.

"He beat Hercules!" sometruck shouts in the crowd.

"That's a bunch of baloney!" another truck argues. "He cheated!"

Theseus can't stay idle any longer.

CHAPTER TWO

BULLISTIC!

Theseus shifts into high gear.

He speeds toward the arena floor.

Theseus hopes to one day become

a ThunderTruck, just like Perseus and

Hercules. ThunderTrucks always help

anytruck in need. The rookie truck must stop

Bullistic from cheating.

But when Theseus reaches the arena floor, the final event is already underway.

The SuperSprint Track!

"Racers get ready!" shouts the announcer.

Eight trucks roll up to the SuperSprint Track starting line.

"ATALANTA! ATALANTA!" the crowd cheers.

Atalanta is the smallest ThunderTruck on the track, but she is also the fastest. Everytruck expects her to win.

"Get set!" the announcer continues.

The racers rev their engines and puffs of smoke spill from their exhaust pipes.

"*Go!*" the announcer yells, waving a green starting flag.

Engines roar!

Tires spin!

Dust fills the air!

When the sky clears, all the racers have sped off — except for Atalanta. She has been knocked on her side.

Bullistic! Theseus thinks. *That evil bully must have rammed her!*

Atalanta quickly gets back on her tires.

FWOOOSH!

She zooms away.

A microsecond later, the miniature ThunderTruck passes one racer. Then she darts between two others.

"Atalanta! Atalanta!" the crowd honks her on.

The trucks speed around a corner. Atalanta blurs passed one truck on the inside and then another on the outside.

On the final straightaway, Atalanta closes in on the SuperSprint Track leader, Bullistic!

Just as Atalanta prepares to pass,

Bullistic's tailgate pops open! Dozens of

nails, screws, and bolts spill out of his truck

bed and into Atalanta's path.

The teeny-tiny

ThunderTruck can't avoid

the ultra-sharp objects. She

drives over

a nail, and – *KA-POW!* – her

front, left tire explodes! She spins off

the racetrack.

"Ooh!" the crowd exhausts.

Moments later, a checkered flag waves

Bullistic across the finish line.

"Bullistic is your new ThunderJam 3000

champion!" the announcer shouts.

The evil monster truck drives onto

the first-place podium. **"BULLISTIC!**

BULLISTIC!" everytruck cheers . . .

except Theseus.

"That no-good bucket of bolts cheated!" Theseus cries out.

The crowd muffles their excitement.

Bullistic bends his shocks and then springs from the podium. He lands in front of Theseus with an earth-shaking *THUD!*

SNORT!

SNORT!

Blistering fireballs blast from his horn-shaped pipes. "Who do you think you are?" Bullistic rumbles.

The rookie truck parks tire to tire with the big-time bully. He stares into Bullistic's red, beady bull's-eyes.

"I am Theseus," he proudly declares.

"Well, Theseus," says Bullistic, "prepare to become . . .

SCRAP METAL!"

CHAPTER THREE
BULLFIGHT

SNNOOORRTT! SNNOOORRTT!

The evil monster truck bullishly revs his engine. Then he wheelies onto his massive back tires, preparing to crush Theseus.

"Hold your horsepower!" honks a truck from behind.

Bullistic and Theseus spin and spot a small purple truck heading toward them.

"Quit flapping your mud flaps, Aria!"

Bullistic shouts at his little sistertruck.

"This is my bullfight!"

"Can't you settle this argument another way?" Aria asks.

"How about a race?" Theseus quickly suggests, knowing he's one of the fastest trucks around.

"Think you can run with this bull, rookie?" Bullistic snorts.

"When and where?" Theseus says, sounding like a true ThunderTruck.

"Tomorrow," Bullistic grunts. "At the

MONSTER MAZE!"

With those words,

everytruck rolls up their

windows and locks

their doors in fear.

No ThunderTruck has ever entered the

Monster Maze and come away with four tires

— except Bullistic.

"Come on, sis!" the evil monster truck

calls after Aria. Bullistic speeds off with his

sistertruck in tow.

Before she disappears, Aria looks back at

Theseus with a sly smile.

That night, Theseus can't stop his engine from running. The Monster Maze will be his greatest challenge yet.

But if the rookie truck wins, he'll surely get upgraded to an official ThunderTruck!

KNOCK!
KNOCK!
KNOCK!

Just then, someone knocks on his garage door. Theseus opens the door, and Aria rolls inside.

"What are you doing here?" Theseus asks her.

"I'm not the same model as my brothertruck," Aria sputters. "I don't like how he wins races."

"Then what do you want?" the rookie truck asks.

"I want to help you win," Aria says.

She opens her tailgate and dumps a shiny, stainless steel winch onto the garage floor.

"What's that for?" Theseus
wonders aloud.

"In case you get stuck," she says, "in
the Monster Maze!"

CHAPTER FOUR

MONSTER MAZE!

The next day, Theseus equips himself with Aria's winch. Then he meets Bullistic atop a hill overlooking the Monster Maze. The course twists and turns for miles and miles into the distance.

A crowd gathers at the maze entrance. Everytruck is there, including his favorite ThunderTrucks, Perseus and Hercules. Theseus spots Aria as well.

Soon, a race official rolls over to the two competitors. "The rules are simple," she tells them. "First one to the middle of the maze — and back — wins!"

The official raises a green starting flag and begins the countdown.

"One!" she yells.

Theseus revs his engine.

"Two!" the official continues her count.

As Theseus expects, Bullistic lets out a deafening blast from his horn-shaped pipes. And once again, no truck hears the official say, **"Three!"** But Bullistic takes off anyway.

Before racing after him, Theseus hooks the winch to a tree near the entrance of the Monster Maze. Then — **FWOOSH!** — he speeds off with the cable unraveling behind him.

Moments later, towering rock walls rise up around the racers. They block out all but a sliver of sunlight.

Theseus follows Bullistic's tracks, but they are difficult to see in the rocky terrain and dim light. Soon, he is lost!

The rookie truck speeds around a corner and skids to a halt.

A dead end!

And then another!

Suddenly, a large shadow looms over him.

 Theseus cries out.

"Do want to know why no truck survives the Monster Maze?" Bullistic asks.

"W-why?" Theseus sputters.

"Because I don't let them escape!" The evil monster truck shoots flames from his pipes, and then charges at Theseus like a mad bull.

Theseus dodges out of the way as Bullistic crashes into the nearby wall.

WHAM! Rocks crack and crumble to the ground.

Bullistic quickly spins around. *"I'll get you!"* he snorts.

But Theseus is already racing away. The rookie truck speeds around another corner and then darts down a long, straight hallway.

As he zooms ahead, Theseus can hear Bullistic closing in behind him. The big-time bully blasts on his horn.

SNNOOOORRTT!

SNNOOOORRTT!

Rocks crunch under his tires. His engine revs angrily.

Then, Theseus hears Bullistic snort with laughter. **_"I've got you now, rookie!"_**

Up ahead, the asphalt suddenly gives way. A large pit opens in the road, filled with spiky, jagged rocks. Behind Theseus, the thick metal bumper of Bullistic closes in on him.

Theseus is stuck between the rocks and very hard place!

CHAPTER FIVE

TRUE CHAMPION

Just then, Theseus recalls what Aria had said the night before. *In case you get stuck,* he thinks, remembering his brand-new winch.

Without a second thought, the rookie truck bends his shocks and . . . leaps into the deep, dark pit! His winch cable unravels, faster and faster, as he plummets toward the jagged rocks below.

"Ahhhhhh!" Theseus shouts.

Then suddenly — **SPROING!** — the

cable pulls tight, and

Theseus stops falling. He

swings back and forth from

his winch like a bungee

jumper.

Below him, Theseus spots old tires,

mufflers, and other rusted-out truck parts

among the rocks. *This must be the center of*

the Monster Maze, he thinks.

Theseus hears laughter above.

"Another one bites my dust!" Bullistic

shouts into the pit.

The megaton monster truck speeds away, leaving a dirty cloud in his wake.

"Time to take this bull by the horns!" Theseus tells himself. The rookie truck recoils his winch, and the cable pulls him from the pit like a fish on a hook.

Back on the road, Theseus knows he must beat Bullistic back to the entrance. But how? The rookie truck is completely lost within the maze!

Suddenly, Theseus spots the winch cable lying on the ground, and his dome light illuminates with an idea.

"Of course!" he exclaims.

Theseus follows the winch cable
back through the maze like a trail of
breadcrumbs. Nearing the entrance, he
finally catches up to Bullistic.

"Looks like I solved your maze!" Theseus
tells his colossal competitor.

"Bull!" Bullistic snorts.
"You've made a HUGE
mistake!"

The evil monster
truck blasts Theseus
with scorching-hot flames.

As Theseus begins to overheat, he notices his winch cable is wrapped around one of Bullistic's tires.

A smile spreads across the rookie truck's front grill. "The bigger they are," he begins, circling Bullistic at superspeed, "the harder they fall!"

Theseus pulls the cable tight as a lasso and — *WHAM-O!* — the big-time bully smashes to the ground. *"NoOooOOooo!"* Bullistic cries.

Moments later, Theseus speeds out of the maze entrance, towing Bullistic behind him.

"Theseus wins!" the official booms.

The crowd gives three honks for the victor.

Aria greets Theseus at the finish line. "You did it! You did it!" she says.

"With your help, of course," Theseus replies. "Thank you."

Then Perseus and Hercules rumble over to the rookie truck.

"You are a true champion, Theseus,"

Perseus tells him.

Hercules nods his hood in agreement. "And

a ThunderTruck from bumper

to bumper!"

Theseus honks his horn with glee.

CHAPTER ONE

BROKEN DOWN

*Putt-putt-putt-***BANG!**
*Putt-putt-putt-***BANG!**

A run-down pickup truck sputters back and forth in front of a repair shop.

Suddenly, the garage door opens. Out rolls the shop's owner, a rough-looking tow truck with a large, dangling winch.

"What's all the racket?" he honks.

"Sorry, Poly-D!" sputters the truck.

Putt-putt-putt-

"What do you need this time, Perseus?"

the owner asks, annoyed.

"What don't I need?" replies the pickup.

"A new transmission, muffler, mud flaps,

rearview mirrors—"

"Your shocks look pretty good," Poly-D interrupts.

"If I'm gonna remain an official ThunderTruck, I need to do more than jump," Perseus explains.

"I'm sure there's something else you can do," says the owner. "Just think about it."

Perseus shakes his hood.

"Well," adds Poly-D, "all those repairs will cost you."

"But I've been running on empty for months," Perseus beeps sadly.

Poly-D shrugs his fenders, and Perseus's front grill bends into a frown.

Just then, Perseus spots something in his headlights. A flyer for the **World Endur-X Championship** hangs on a wall of the shop.

It is the longest, and possibly most the dangerous, race ever.

Competitors start in the city of Trolympia.

They race over a towering mountain, across

a bottomless bog, and through an endless

desert to the end of the world — and

back again.

The flyer says the winner will receive free

repairs for a year!

"I will be back!" Perseus

says, determined.

Putt-putt-putt-BANG!

CHAPTER TWO
THE ENDUR-X CHAMPIONSHIP

The next day, Perseus sputters into

Trolympia. *Putt-putt-putt-* **BANG!**

The city's rocky streets are already

crowded with fully fueled race fans. They

wave colorful banners in support of their

favorite ThunderTrucks.

"HERCULES! HERCULES!"

Some trucks honk.

"B-PHON! B-PHON!"

Others beep.

Perseus follows the other trucks toward the Endur-X Championship starting line.

"HONK!" A race official suddenly blares at the pickup truck. "Only fully repaired ThunderTrucks are allowed in this race."

Perseus believes his plan has already backfired. Just then, the sellout crowd revs with excitement.

"ARGONUTZ! ARGONUTZ!"

Perseus spins on his wheels and spots Argonutz 'N Bolts. The popular ThunderTruck's golden fenders sparkle in the sunlight.

Behind him, an evil monster truck slowly approaches. Puffs of gray smoke billow from her dent-covered hood. She is a real rust bucket!

"Who's that?" Perseus asks the security guard.

CRUNNNNNCH!

The mysterious monster truck suddenly slams into Argonutz's rear bumper.

THUNK!

His golden fenders instantly crash to the ground, and the ThunderTruck stalls before reaching the starting line.

The official shifts into high gear.

"Medusa!" he exclaims, rattling with fear. "Best stay away from her! She's a real gas guzzler!"

"What do you mean?" Perseus asks.

"One fender bender with her could suck the life out of anytruck!" he says.

Then

The official puts pedal to metal and speeds off.

Perseus thinks about doing the same, but he knows this is his only shot at entering the race.

*Putt-putt-putt-***BANG!**

He sputters up to the starting line.

"I didn't know you were coming," another truck asks him. It is Theseus, the first to conquer the Monster Maze.

"I . . . um . . . Argonutz couldn't make it," Perseus tells him. "I'm taking his place."

"Just don't think you're going to beat me!" Atalanta blares from her position at the starting line. Everytruck knows she's the fastest truck in the world!

Looking down the starting line, Perseus also spots Hercules and B-Phon. He sees a giant truck called Bullistic and another known as Hydra. Then there's Cyclops, a truck with only one headlight, and a mean-looking truck called The Boar.

Ten racers in all.

Perseus thinks he doesn't stand a chance!

Moments later —

Baaaaawoooogaaahhh! — a loud horn blows. The race official returns. "Racers take your mark," he sputters, keeping a close headlight on Medusa.

"Get set . . ."

VROOOOOOM! Engines roar.

RUMMBLE! The ground shakes.

Everytruck cheers.

"Go!" the official declares.

Knobby tires spin on the gravel, and the

trucks dart forward.

CRUNNNNNCH!

Before the trucks even reach second gear,

Medusa rams Cyclops! His lone headlight

cracks and falls to the ground. Then —

POOF! — a puff of smoke billows out from

under his hood.

Seconds later, **SMAAAASH!** Medusa crashes into B-Phon, and his tires instantly go flat.

"Hey!" B-phon says too late. "No fair!"

Just like that, the race is down to eight trucks!

CHAPTER THREE

MOUNTAIN MADNESS

Perseus speeds past the broken-down

Cyclops and B-phon. All around him,

row upon row of trucks line the Endur-X

Championship course.

Through the crowd, Perseus spots the

towering Mount Trolympus in the distance. It

will be their first big obstacle!

Suddenly, a giant,
flame-red monster
truck steers toward
Perseus.

Thick, black smoke spews from two

horn-shaped pipes on the vehicle's hood.

Bullistic is headed straight for him!

WHAM-O! Before he can reach

Perseus, Medusa slams into Bullistic.

His flame-red paint job instantly rusts,

and his engine stalls.

Then Medusa turns her evil headlights on Atalanta. The World's Fastest Truck tries to get out of the way. But Medusa rams into Atalanta's side.

SMAAAAASH!

Suddenly, all four of Atalanta's tires fly off and roll away. **THUD!**

Her body lands on the dirt and smoke pours out from under her hood.

A nervous air bubble builds in Perseus' gas line. "Only six racers left," he gulps.

Mount Trolympus rises in front of Perseus. Some of the other racers have already reached its base. They zoom up a winding canyon that leads toward the top. Perseus follows in their dusty tire tracks.

As he speeds along, two large shadows suddenly cross his path. Then he hears a loud **BOOM** and feels the ground shake and rumble.

Ahead, on the path, a large boulder tumbles down the mountainside.

It rolls back and forth down the path.

As it nears Perseus, he spots small pile of rocks off to the side. He races over them and leaps into the air.

Perseus sails safely over the boulder as it

crashes down the hill.

Where did that come from? he thinks.

A little farther up the mountain, Perseus

sees Hydra. One side of the canyon wall has

collapsed on him. The evil truck is buried

under a pile of dirt and rocks!

"What happened?" Perseus asks.

"I don't know," Hydra rumbles. "A boulder just fell out of the sky!"

"Do you need help?" Perseus asks.

"NO!" Hydra growls. "Not from a beat-up ThunderTruck!"

Perseus races away, but he looks back to make sure Hydra gets out okay.

He sees Medusa racing up to Hydra.

Hydra is still pinned under the rocks when Medusa rams into him.

Hydra's tires stop spinning, and his engine starts to *wheeze* and *cough*. Then his headlights flicker and dim.

Medusa keeps chugging up the mountain.

Only five racers remain — and Medusa is right on Perseus's mud flaps!

CHAPTER FOUR

THE GORGONATERS!

When Perseus reaches the top of
Mount Trolympus, he sees the other racers.
Medusa chugs up the mountain behind him.
Ahead of him, Hercules, Theseus, and
The Boar speed down the other side of
the mountain.

With his jumping ability, Perseus hopes he can catch up to them. He races over a small berm and leaps into the air.

FWOOOSH!

He soars part way down the mountain.

Then he races over a larger berm —

FWOOOSH! — and he sails even farther

down!

Perseus catches up to the other racers

at the bottom of the mountain. But he

only sees Hercules and The Boar. They are

stopped in the middle of the road.

Perseus rolls up to them.

"What's wrong?" he sputters.

"Sometruck dug a pit in the middle of the

track," The Boar rumbles.

In front of them, there is a large hole. At

the bottom of it is Theseus!

"Are you okay?" Hercules yells down

to him.

"Think I have

a sprained axle,"

Theseus blares.

"You'll have to go on

without me."

Now only four racers remain!

"What do we do?" Perseus asks.

Just then, a familiar

sputtering and chugging

comes from behind him.

They all turn to see

Medusa.

"Let's get out of here!"

Hercules honks.

The ThunderTruck climbs over some boulders on the side of the pit. The Boar tries to follow, but the rocks shift under the gigantic truck's weight.

Perseus is not much of a climber. He is a jumper. He backs up to get a running start. His engine revs, his tires spin, and then he takes off. As he nears the edge of the pit, he leaps into the air.

Perseus soars over the pit and lands with a **THUMP** on the other side.

He stops to look back. Hercules is almost past the pit. But The Boar is stuck on the other side.

Medusa rolls up to him and gives him a nudge. All of The Boar's doors fall off. His lights flicker. Then his engine *hiccups* and coughs a puff of smoke.

"Get going!" Hercules shouts to Perseus.

With only three racers left, Perseus takes the lead!

Up ahead, Perseus discovers the next obstacle — a bubbling and oily bog!

Through the bog lies a twisty dirt path.

Perseus glances back to see if Hercules is following him. What he sees frightens him. As Hercules speeds around one twist in the path, a dark shadow swoops down. It rams into him. **KA-BLAM!** Hercules almost slides off the path!

Then as Hercules races around a curve, another dark shadow dives down. It crashes into Hercules, and he flies off the path. With a *SPLOOSH*, he lands in the bubbling oil and is stuck.

Now the race is down to just Perseus and Medusa!

On the other side of the bog lies the final obstacle — endless desert! Sandy dunes stretch out as far as he can see.

Perseus stops to take a break. He looks back and sees the large, shadowy shapes towing Medusa across bog. They set her down on the other side.

"Who are they?" Perseus asks.

"The Gorgonaters!" Medusa blares.

"These monster trucks are exactly like me — with one upgrade. They can jump even higher than you!"

"We dropped that boulder on Hydra," one Gorgonater rumbles.

"We dug the pit that trapped Theseus," the other grumbles.

"And now we will get you!" they squeal together.

Perseus takes off! His tires spin in the loose sand.

Putt-putt-putt-**BANG!**
Putt-putt-putt-**BANG!**

He cannot go very fast, and the Gorgonaters are right behind him.

Up ahead, Perseus spots a large dune, and a smile spreads across his grill. He has an idea!

Perseus speeds up it — faster and faster — forcing the Gorgonaters to follow. "It's not how high you can jump—" he honks back at the evil trucks.

FWOOOOOOOSH!

He soars off the dune like a ramp, and the Gorgonaters do the same.

WHUMP! Perseus lands safely on the other side. "It's how well you land on your wheels," he finishes.

CRASH!

WHOOOOMP!!

The Gorgonaters spiral out of control and land engine-deep in the sand.

"NOooOOooO!" Medusa cries. Only she and Perseus remain.

CHAPTER FIVE

BEYOND REPAIR

As Perseus speeds through the desert, grayness surrounds him. The path narrows, and the ground drops away on either side. He races along a thinning ledge until the land ends at a narrow point. He has reached the end of the world.

Perseus rolls up the edge of the cliff and peers down.

There is only grayness below and only grayness ahead. He is surrounded by grayness, except for the path he just drove down.

"I've got you now," Medusa rattles.

Perseus spins around.

Medusa blocks his path.

Perseus knows he cannot let her touch him. But there is no way around her. And the path here is flat. He does not have even the tiniest of bumps to use to leap over her.

But Perseus has a thought. Medusa is always chasing after other trucks, and they are always running away scared. Maybe he needs to give *her* a scare.

Perseus revs his engine. He spins his tires, kicking up a cloud of dust.

"What . . . are . . . you . . . doing?" Medusa gasps.

"I'm going to ram you off the path," he honks.

Then Perseus screeches toward her. Medusa's headlights flicker in fear. She backs away.

As she does, one of her tires slips off the narrow ledge. It *whirs* and it spins in the air.

Perseus now has just enough room to get by her. He swerves around her, with his tires on the edge of the ledge.

He races by her and speeds back through the endless desert. He weaves around the twisty and curvy path through the bottomless bog. He climbs up and over the towering Mount Trolympus.

Then he races through the streets of Trolympia and back into the arena. Fans honk as he crosses the finishes line.

"And the winner is," the race official
shouts in disbelief, **"Perseus!"**
Putt-putt-putt-BANG!

After receiving his prize, Perseus returns to Poly-D's Repair & Salvage Shop. What he finds there surprises him!

Several trucks are outside. There is Jason with his fender attached, and B-phon has a new bumper. Atalanta, Hercules, and Theseus are also fixed.

Off to the side are the evil monster trucks — all of them except for Medusa. They are testing out their new repairs.

Perseus rolls up to the garage. He sees Poly-D working on a beat-up truck up on the lift. Then Perseus recognizes who is up on the lift. **Medusa!**

"Stay away from her!"

Perseus warns.

"Why? Medusa's my best customer," Poly-D says. "It could take days . . . weeks . . . maybe years to fix everything wrong with her."

Perseus rolls back outside. He is joined by all the ThunderTrucks.

"What are you doing here anyway?" Theseus asks. "You won the race."

"Exactly," Perseus replies. "I'm using the prize to finally get the repairs I need."

"You're beyond repair!" Hercules says.

Perseus's grill folds into a frown. He'll never remain an official ThunderTruck, he thinks.

Then B-Phon says, "He means, you can't fix what isn't broken."

"Really?" Perseus's headlights beam brightly.

The others rev their engines. "Once a ThunderTruck, always a ThunderTruck!" they say.

Putt-putt-putt-BANG!

CHAPTER ONE

MIGHTIEST TRUCK ON EARTH

A giant ThunderTruck rumbles down a

rocky road. Its engines roar.

VROOM! VROOM! VROOM!

When the ThunderTruck spots a deep bog,

he puts pedal to metal.

WHOOSH!

His tires spin and kick up muck until he reaches the other side.

When the ThunderTruck sees a boulder no one can budge, he hooks up his ultra-strong winch. With a tremendous tug, he pulls until the rock lets loose.

CRUNNNCH!

When he sees a rocky cliff that no one has climbed, the truck zooms up it with

MAXIMUM HORSEPOWER!

Then the super-size truck blares, "I am Hercules — mightiest truck ever built!"

It is true! The mighty Hercules can out-pull and out-haul everytruck.

There is no obstacle he hasn't conquered. No challenge that frightens him. Except for one: his yearly tune up!

SCREEEEEECH!

Just then, Hercules squeals to a stop outside Poly-D's Repair & Salvage Shop. The mighty vehicle is surprised to see other ThunderTrucks waiting, including his ThunderJam competitors, Perseus and Theseus.

Hercules notices his friend has a flat! "Perseus, what happened?" he asks.

"I tried completing the Rough & Tough Twelve," Perseus puffed.

"Me, too," honks Theseus. "That's how my grill got mangled!"

"What's the Rough & Tough Twelve?" Hercules asks.

Perseus replies, "Only the toughest—"

"And the roughest!" interrupts Theseus.

"—obstacles on Earth!" Perseus finishes.

"What types of obstacles?"

"They are different for every truck," Perseus says. "The Royal Rumbler picks the obstacles."

"He owns the decal shop in Trolympia," Theseus adds.

Hercules asks, "What happens if I conquer all twelve obstacles?"

"You get a decal that says **World's Mightiest Truck**," says Perseus.

BEEP! BEEP! Hercules honks with glee. He already knows he's the mightiest truck on Earth, but the decal would make it official!

Just then, one by one, the other trucks go into the shop for repairs.

"Hercules!" Poly-D, the shop's owner, shouts. "Ready for your tune-up?"

"I am," Hercules blares. "I'm ready for anything!"

"Then open your hood and say *ahhhh*," Poly-D says.

"Anything but that!"

Hercules rattles in fear.

CHAPTER TWO

THE ROYAL RUMBLER

The next day, Hercules rolls into the Royal

Rumbler's Decal Shop.

"Hercules!" the Royal Rumbler shouts.

"You are the—"

"Mightiest truck alive!"

Hercules revs excitedly.

Hercules glances around the shop. Behind the counter, he sees the sticker he wants. The one his friends told him about. In big, gold, swirly letters, it reads, **"World's Mightiest Truck."**

"Or I will be," Hercules adds. "Once I get that decal!"

"You can't buy that decal," the Royal Rumbler explains. "It's one of a kind. You must earn it."

"How do I do that?" Hercules asks.

"Complete my Rough & Tough Twelve," the Royal Rumbler replies. "Then it is yours."

"I am up for any challenge!" Hercules blares. "What's my first obstacle?"

"Pick up my mail from the post office," the Royal Rumbler says.

"That sounds like a chore—" Hercules starts to say.

The Royal Rumbler interrupts. "If it is too tough for you, I can find another ThunderTruck."

"I'll do it." Hercules revs his engine. In a cloud of dust, he zooms off.

VROOOOOOOM!

At the post office, a mound of mail rises up to the sky.

"Is that all for the Royal Rumbler?" Hercules asks.

"Yup," the mail truck says. "He hasn't picked it up a year!"

"Okay, load me up," Hercules blares.

A crane drops a pile of mail into Hercules's truck bed.

"Oompf!" he honks under the weight. "I hope I don't strain an axle."

putt! putt! putt!

He sputters back to the Royal Rumbler. After that load, Hercules goes back for another and another and another. It takes all day!

"Whew! I'm exhausted," Hercules says.

POOF! A puff of black exhaust shoots out his tail pipe.

But more challenges await! The Royal Rumbler orders Hercules to trucksit his nephew, buy him a set of golden hubcaps, and clean out his garage. And there's more!

After the sixth obstacle, Hercules revs his engine angrily.

The Rough & Tough Twelve isn't like he'd imagined. He wasn't leaping flaming tires or racing through deadly canyons. Nothing fun!

"You're just having me do your chores!" Hercules tells the Royal Rumbler.

"They have been tough, haven't they?" the Royal Rumbler asks.

"Well, yes," Hercules admits.

"And rough?"

"Okay, yes," begins Hercules. "But how will they make me the Mightiest Truck on Earth?" he asks. "No one cares if I can haul your mail or clean out a garage."

"Do you give up then?" the Royal Rumbler asks.

"Of course not!" Hercules rumbles.

"Good," the Royal Rumbler says, "because notruck has ever completed my next obstacle!"

CHAPTER THREE
HYDRA

"For your seventh obstacle, you will face . . . **HYDRA!**" the Royal Rumbler says. "This mean monster truck lives in the Bottomless Bog."

Hercules knows the oily bog is a dangerous place. A twisty and curvy trail winds its ways through the bog.

Anyone who misses one of the turns risks sliding into the muck and sinking into the bog's bottomless depths.

"And if you beat Hydra," the Royal Rumbler adds, "I want you to bring me his tire rims."

"Are you sure this isn't another chore?" Hercules asks.

"Just go!" the Royal Rumbler beeps.

Hercules drives around Mount Trolympus to reach the Bottomless Bog. As he rolls along its windy path, a large truck leaps out in front of him.

But it is not any ordinary truck! Instead of just four wheels, it has four wheels on each side. Plus, a ninth wheel in front.

"Hydra!" Hercules roars.

"No one passes through the Bottomless Bog without paying a toll," Hydra rumbles. "I need one of your tires."

Just behind Hydra, Hercules sees a stack of tires piled up. Off to both sides of the path lie beat up and smashed trucks with only three wheels.

"Not a chance!" Hercules says.

"Then I will take all of your tires!" Hydra honks.

VROOOSH! Hydra's engine roars.

The big truck spins all nine tires and rushes Hercules.

Hercules meets his charge, ramming into Hydra's front tire.

POP! The tire bursts.

But that does not stop Hydra! The mean monster truck revs his engine and pushes Hercules toward the oily bog!

Hercules' engine screams, and he shoves Hydra back. Hydra lands on one of the nearby wrecks. **POP!** Another one of Hydra's tires bursts.

"*RAWR!*" Hydra roars. The monster

truck's tires spin as he rams into Hercules.

But Hercules is the mightiest truck alive.

He digs in, kicking up muck and dirt, and he

pushes back.

POP! Another of Hydra's tires bursts.

Each time Hydra pushes, Hercules shoves back. **POP! POP! POP! *POPPITY! POP!***

THUD! After all of Hydra's tires pop, his chassis slams into the ground.

Using his winch, Hercules then yanks off four of Hydra's tires.

"Impressive," the Royal Rumbler says when Hercules arrives back at his shop. "Are you ready for the eighth obstacle?"

"Yes!" Hercules beeps. "That last one was fun!"

"Then challenge The Boar to a tug-o-war match!" the Royal Rumbler says. "And bring me his bumper."

CHAPTER FOUR
THE BOAR AND MORE!

A short time later, Hercules finds The
Boar in a large field. The monster truck is
dragging a smaller truck around and around.
As he zips around, pieces of the other trucks
fall off and fly everywhere. Hercules feels
sorry for the small truck.

"Pick on someone your own size!"

Hercules roars.

SCRRREEEEEECH! The Boar

screeches to a halt.

"Are you challenging me?" he rumbles.

"Yes, to a tug-of-war

match!" Hercules replies.

The two hook up a chain to

their hitches.

"On the count of three, we

pull," The Boar says. **"One!"**

VROOOM! VROOM! The trucks rev

their engines.

"Two," The Boar shouts.

Before shouting out *"three,"* The

Boar lurches forward. He starts to drag

Hercules across the field. But Hercules digs

in and tugs back.

The two trucks yank

and pull.

Tires spin!

Engines roar!

Dust flies!

As Hercules and The Boar jerk each other

back and forth, they dig ruts into the ground.

Back and forth they tug, spinning their tires.

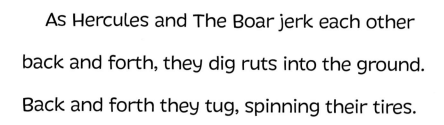

The ruts turn into a deep ditch. Then a trench.

Hercules worries he could get stuck. So he veers to the right, climbs up over a berm, and speeds out of the deepening hole. He drags The Boar behind him.

The Boar gets hung up on the berm, with all four of his tires spinning in the air.

Then Hercules gives one last mighty yank. **SCCCRRRRREEECCHH!**

He rips The Boar's back bumper off.

"Amazing!" the Royal Rumbler says when Hercules delivers the bumper.

"For your ninth obstacle, race the Chimera Brothers. And bring me back one of their engines."

Hercules quickly finds the three Chimera Brothers near a racetrack just outside of town. The Lion has teeth like spikes on his front bumper. He races up behind a truck and bites its back tires. **POP! POP!** The other truck spins out.

The Goat, which has a battering ram sticking out of his grill, runs into the helpless truck. It tips over. The Dragon rolls up to the truck. He shoots a jet of flame from its grill, blackening the helpless truck.

"Stop that!"

Hercules shouts as he rumbles over to them.

"But he lost the race," The Goat screeches.

"Do you want to take his place?" The Lion roars.

"Yes, let's race," The Dragon snarls, a blast of flame shooting out from under his hood.

"Okay," Hercules says. "But if I win, I get one of your engines."

"And if you lose, we roast you," The Dragon says.

Hercules and the Chimera Brothers roll up to the starting line.

"On the count of three," The Goat screeches.

But Hercules knows what will happen. So once the count reaches "two," he takes off.

At the same time, The Goat and The Lion try to smash into him. But since Hercules took off early, the two Chimera Brothers crash into each other. Parts go flying everywhere.

That leaves just The Dragon. He looks terrified.

"Okay, here, just take it," he says, popping his hood.

Hercules grabs The Dragon's engine and heads back to the decal shop.

"Incredible!" the Royal Rumbler honks. "For the tenth obstacle, I want you to race Bullistic through the Labyrinth! And bring me one of his horns."

Upon returning with Bullistic's horn, the Royal Rumbler says, "Astounding! For the eleventh obstacle, race the giant Atlas up Mount Trolympus. And bring me back his grill."

For each task, Hercules does what he's asked. When he is done, he has a pile of tires, bumpers, and other spare parts piled up.

"What are you going to do with all of these?" Hercules asks.

"Come back tomorrow, and you'll find out," the Royal Rumbler says.

CHAPTER FIVE

IT'S OFFICIAL

The next day, Hercules drives up to the Royal Rumbler's shop. All sorts of loud noises come from inside.

Hercules hears the **krik krik krik** of a wrench. There is the **vrrrttt vrrrttt** of an air gun. Then the **WHOOSH** a of lift is followed by the thud of four tires hitting the floor.

Hercules rolls through the door.

"What's going on—?" he stops.

The Royal Rumbler stands next the oddest-looking truck that Hercules has ever seen. It is made from all the parts that Hercules had gathered for the Royal Rumbler.

"Who is that?" Hercules asks.

"This is The Mutt," the Royal Rumbler says proudly.

"What does he have to do with my last obstacle?" Hercules asks.

"Simple," the Royal Rumbler begins, "destroy you —

because the World's Mightiest Truck decal is mine. All mine!"

The monstrous

truck revs his engines.
VRRRVRRRMMM!

"Uh-oh!" Hercules turns and speeds

out the door. The Mutt roars after him.

But he is too big to fit through the door.

SMAAAAASH! He crashes through

the wall!

Hercules then zooms through the city streets. The Mutt roars after him.

Outside of town, Hercules drives up a hill. He flies over it like a ramp and lands with a thud!

The Mutt flies over the hill. He lands with an earthshaking **THUMP!**

Hercules races along a road through a forest. The Mutt plows through the trees.

Hercules twists and winds his way through the Bottomless Bog. The Mutt speeds right through the mucky oil.

No matter what Hercules does, he cannot lose the monstrous truck.

"Doesn't he know I am the mightiest truck alive?" Hercules wonders aloud.

The Mutt rams Hercules from behind.

"I guess not!" Hercules beeps.

Hercules and The Mutt race around and
around. They fly over hills. They
spin their tires through oily bogs.
They hop over sandy dunes. They
circle around the towering Mount
Trolympus.

Hercules starts to sputter and chug.

"I'm running out of gas," he beeps.

But The Mutt has an extra-large tank. The
words Geyron's Gas are written on it.

"I need to do something quick," Hercules
whispers to himself.

He thinks, *The Mutt is made up of put-together parts. Maybe I can take him apart.*

As Hercules whirls around a huge rock, he lets out the chain from his winch. The Mutt drives over it, and the chain catches on his front axle. Going around and around the rock, The Mutt gets so tangled in the chain that his front wheels get torn off.

The Mutt goes flying and flips over. His remaining tires spin in the air, and he lets loose a loud blast from his horn.

HHOONNKK!!

"Now's my chance!" Hercules beeps.

Hercules quickly hooks up his chain
to The Mutt's back bumper. He gives a
tremendous yank. **SCREECH!** It rips off.
"RAWR!" The Mutt honks as black
exhaust shoots out of his tailpipe.

Piece by spare part, Hercules takes The Mutt apart. All that is left of the monstrous truck is a heap of junk.

"The decal is mine!" Hercules honks proudly.

After completing the Rough & Tough Twelve, Hercules wants to show off his new decal. He drives by Poly-D's Repair & Salvage Shop hoping to see if some of his friends are there.

"Whatcha got there?" Poly-D calls to him.

"It's a new decal," Hercules replies.

"Not that. What are you hauling?" Poly-D asks. "Can I give it a free tune up?"

In his bed, Hercules has all the parts from the other monster trucks parts that he took for the Royal Rumbler.

"What do you want with this junk?" Hercules asks.

Poly-D rolls aside so that Hercules can see into his shop. Up on one lift is Hydra, with no wheels. On another lift is The Boar, missing his rear end. Off to the side, he sees the Chimera Brothers.

The Lion and The Goat are banged up and dented. The Dragon's hood is open, and he has no engine. There is a hornless Bullistic and Atlas without his grill.

"My new customers could use them," Poly-D beeps.

Hercules dumps the load in front of the shop.

"It's all yours," he says to Poly-D. "And schedule me for a tune up next week."

"Really?" Poly-D asks.

"Yeah, the mechanic can't be any worse than doing the Royal Rumbler's chores!"

BLAKE HOENA

Blake Hoena grew up in central Wisconsin, where he wrote stories about robots conquering the moon and trolls lumbering around the woods behind his parents house. He now lives in St. Paul, Minnesota, with his wife, two kids, a dog, and a couple of cats. Blake continues to make up stories about things like space aliens and superheroes, and he has written more than 70 chapter books and graphic novels for children.

FERN CANO

Fernando Cano is an emerging illustrator born in Mexico City, Mexico. He currently resides in Monterrey, Mexico, where he works as a full-time illustrator and colorist at Graphikslava studio. He has done illustration work for Marvel, DC Comics, and role-playing games like Pathfinder from Paizo Publishing. In his spare time, he enjoys hanging out with friends, singing, rowing, and drawing.